Bullies
Rule

Bullies Rule

Monique Polak

Orca currents

ORCA BOOK PUBLISHERS

Library and Archives Canada Cataloguing in Publication

Polak, Monique, author
Bullies rule / Monique Polak.
(Orca currents)

Issued in print and electronic formats.
ISBN 978-1-4598-1438-7 (paperback).—ISBN 978-1-4598-1439-4 (pdf).—
ISBN 978-1-4598-1440-0 (epub)

I. Title. II. Series: Orca currents
PS8631.O43B54 2017   jc813'.6   c2016-904474-2
c2016-904475-0

First published in the United States, 2017
Library of Congress Control Number: 2016950077

Summary: In this high-interest novel for middle readers, Daniel is forced to
examine his own behavior after the teasing of a classmate gets out of hand.

*Orca Book Publishers is dedicated to preserving the environment and has
printed this book on Forest Stewardship Council® certified paper.*

Orca Book Publishers gratefully acknowledges the support for its
publishing programs provided by the following agencies: the Government
of Canada through the Canada Book Fund and the Canada Council
for the Arts,and the Province of British Columbia through
the BC Arts Council and the Book Publishing Tax Credit.

Cover photography by iStock.com
Author photo by Monique Dykstra

ORCA BOOK PUBLISHERS
www.orcabook.com

Printed and bound in Canada.

20 19 18 17 • 4 3 2 1

For Robin and Amanda Petrogiannis,
big readers and great friends

Chapter One

I don't mean to be mean.

But I can't resist an opportunity.

Like this morning, during recess, I am hanging in the schoolyard with my buds, and Nelson Wong walks by. His eyes are glued to the asphalt. Guys like me make guys like Nelson nervous.

Let me be clear. I don't have anything against Nelson. It's not his fault he's a math genius or that he's skinnier than a rake. Today he happens to be wearing these baggy gray trackpants. They are practically falling off his bony butt.

Those pants are my opportunity.

I grin when I see Nelson pull up his pants. Then I turn to Trevor and Luke and say, "Watch this, guys!"

Trevor snorts in anticipation. Most kids laugh. Trevor snorts. Luke, who believes that nothing happens until it gets posted on YouTube, whips his cell phone out of his back pocket.

I jog over to where Nelson is huddled with a group of math geniuses. They are probably discussing ratios and right angles, so Nelson doesn't realize I am behind him.

That's when I *pants* him.

It doesn't take much effort. I just grab the elasticized band at the top of his trackpants and give a little tug. Two seconds later, Nelson's knobby knees are knocking together and his trackpants are around his ankles.

What I never expected—and what makes the whole thing even funnier— is that Nelson is wearing red-and-blue Superman boxer shorts. Even the other math nerds fall over laughing.

Nelson hikes up his pants, but it is too late. The whole schoolyard is hooting.

I hear Tanya before I see her. She is singing the chorus of Five for Fighting's "Superman" song: "*I'm more than a bird, I'm more than a plane…*" Now I spot her standing by the fence. Tanya Leboff is the hottest girl in eighth grade. I've had a thing for her since elementary school. Most girls with eyes that blue have blond hair, but Tanya's hair is so dark it is almost black. Not surprisingly, her two sidekicks, Evie and Lily, are singing along with her.

Of course, Luke catches the whole thing on video. When Luke moves in for a close-up, Nelson covers his face with his hands. I guess he isn't ready for his YouTube debut. If I were a different sort of person, I might feel sorry for old Nelson.

I clap when Tanya and the sidekicks finish their song and take a bow. Tanya flips her hair away from her face. She shoots me a smile so small I wonder if I imagined it.

"You're the man," Trevor says, high-fiving me.

I am still shaking my head, picturing those Superman boxer shorts, when I hear the sound of high heels clattering in the distance. Shoes like that belong to only one person. It is Ms. Fornello, our guidance counselor.

When I look up, she is surveying the schoolyard. Luke slips his phone into his pocket.

Her eyes land on me. "Daniel Abel," she says. "Are you going to tell me what's going on here?"

"Uh, nothing's going on, Ms. Fornello." I make a point of looking her in the eye. Most kids can't do that— look someone in the eye and lie to their face. I'm not most kids.

"In that case," Ms. Fornello says, turning to Luke, "you won't mind showing me whatever it is you just recorded on your phone."

"Uh, it was no big deal," Luke says, backing away from Ms. Fornello. "Daniel was just kidding around."

I glare at Luke. Why'd he have to mention my name?

Ms. Fornello is the pit bull of guidance counselors. When she gets an idea, she won't let go. So I am not surprised when she extends her hand. "Your phone," she says to Luke. "Now."

Luke sighs as he hands her the phone. Then he looks at me and mouths the words *Sorry, dude.*

Ms. Fornello curls her index finger in front of my face. "Daniel," she says, "I'll be waiting in my office. I believe it's time for another chat."

"Yes, ma'am," I tell her.

There is no point arguing with a pit bull.

Chapter Two

When I get to her office, Ms. Fornello is watching the video on Luke's phone. I wonder if she's gotten to the part where you see Nelson's Superman boxer shorts. I bet even Ms. Fornello will find that funny.

"I was just kidding around," I say from the doorway.

Ms. Fornello does not lift her eyes from the small screen. I'm hoping it's because she is enjoying the show. "That's what you always say, Daniel," she says in a tired voice. Then she puts down the phone and points to the chair in front of her desk.

"The problem is that for a boy like Nelson Wong, it doesn't feel like *kidding around*. It probably feels more like *utter humiliation*." Ms. Fornello leaves those last two words hanging in the air like a bad smell.

I know where this conversation is headed. Ms. Fornello's favorite word is *empathy,* and she is concerned that I suffer from something called *empathy deficit*. Apparently, bullies, as well as certain politicians, are afflicted by this condition. I have heard it all school year. The first time was when I got sent to Ms. Fornello's office for imitating this guy Jason in gym class who kept missing the basketball net. Then again at the end of September, when I teased Ronnie about his acne. That was no big deal. All I did was nudge Trevor and say, *We could play connect the dots on that dude's face.* But I guess Ronnie can't take a joke, because he went to Ms. Fornello about his hurt feelings.

I'm getting familiar with Ms. Fornello's office décor. The mountain of file folders on her desk, the spider plant hanging in the window, the poster of a hairy caterpillar with the words *Change is Possible* on the wall.

Ms. Fornello has set her sights on changing me. In addition to trying to get me to be more empathic (*How do you think it* feels, *Daniel, to be bad at basketball? And to have someone point it out in front of all your classmates?* and *Can you* imagine, *Daniel, how self-conscious Ronnie might be about his acne?*), Ms. Fornello enjoys nosing around about my family life. After the basketball incident, she wanted to know if someone in my house bullies me. *One of your parents, perhaps? Or an older sibling?* I can't tell you how disappointed she looked when I told her no one does.

After my connect-the-dots crack, Ms. Fornello had wanted to probe deeper into my past. Had I been the victim of bullying in kindergarten or elementary school? When I told her I hadn't, she said, *Some people block out traumatic events as a way to cope.*

To unblock me, Ms. Fornello asked me to close my eyes while she spoke to me in a soothing voice. *I want you to remember back, Daniel…*I think she was trying to hypnotize me, but that did not work either. No traumatic experiences rose to the surface of my mind, though I did get a nice nap and I missed most of math class.

Today, Ms. Fornello surprises me. She does not ask me to imagine what it feels like to be an Asian math nerd wearing Superman boxer shorts in front of the whole school. Or to try and remember if the newborn baby in the incubator next to mine looked at me funny—or hurt my feelings in any way.

I just sit on the hard-backed chair in front of Ms. Fornello's desk, wondering how long she is going to keep me before she sends me to Principal Owen's office.

That part is not going to be fun. Unlike Ms. Fornello, Principal Owen has no interest in subjects like *empathy deficit* or *buried traumatic memories*. Principal Owen is interested in only one thing—punishment.

Old-fashioned detentions do not satisfy him. Principal Owen is more creative than that. He believes in tailoring the punishment to the offense. For example, my basketball imitation landed me an afternoon in the gym, scrubbing the exercise mats. And let me tell you, it had been at least a decade since anyone had taken a sponge to those suckers.

The punishment for my zit comment was worse. Owen made me do three days of after-school community service at a local daycare. I was only allowed to play endless rounds of connect the dots with a series of sneezing, giggling three-year-olds.

I am wondering what kind of punishment Owen will devise when he finds out I pantsed Nelson Wong. I have a hunch he will work in the Superman angle. Maybe he'll make me wear Superman boxer shorts while I rake the leaves in the schoolyard or clean the graffiti off the back wall. What were those words Ms. Fornello used before? *Utter humiliation.* Something tells me that's what Owen will aim for.

Ms. Fornello is watching me in a way that makes me uncomfortable. Like I'm some specimen in a petri dish—a cell she is hoping to culture. A cell she is hoping to *grow*. I look up at the poster of the hairy caterpillar.

I am the one to break the silence. "So are you gonna call Principal Owen or what?" I ask.

"Actually," Ms. Fornello says, "I thought we'd walk over to his office."

"You're coming?" I say. "Don't tell me you're in trouble too."

The corners of Ms. Fornello's lips lift, and for a second I think she is about to smile. But then her lips resume their usual sour position. "Are you ready, Daniel?" she asks.

"Shouldn't you phone first to say we're on our way?" I suggest.

This time Ms. Fornello smiles for real. "That won't be necessary. Principal Owen is expecting us."

Something is up. I know because when we walk into Principal Owen's office he does not mention the pantsing incident. Instead, he gets up from behind his desk and reaches out to shake my hand. *Shake my hand?*

"What's going on here exactly?" I can't help asking. "Aren't I in trouble?" I stop myself from mentioning pantsing. Just in case, by some miracle, Ms. Fornello has decided not to turn me in.

"It's good to see you, Daniel," Principal Owen says.

Good to see me? None of this makes any sense.

Principal Owen sees that I am confused. "Yes, good to see you," he says again. "Ms. Fornello and I wanted to be together when we offered you a new position."

"New position?" So I was right. My new position is going to be chief leaf raker or graffiti remover. My uniform will be Superman boxer shorts.

But that isn't how things go down.

Principal Owen invites me to sit. Not on the usual chair for students receiving punishment. But on his plaid sofa, next to Ms. Fornello.

"The Mountview High School open house is coming up at the end of November," Principal Owen says. "We'd like you to be one of the school's official greeters. You'll be one of the first people parents and potential students meet when they walk into Mountview High."

I look from Principal Owen to Ms. Fornello, then back to Principal Owen. "Is this some kind of joke?"

Principal Owen cracks his knuckles. "I think you know, Daniel, that I'm not the joking type."

Chapter Three

Before she sends me back to class, Ms. Fornello deletes the video from Luke's phone. "You can return this to Luke," she says, tossing me the phone. "And congratulations on your new position, Daniel. You must be very proud."

I check Ms. Fornello's face for signs of sarcasm—but I don't find any.

"Thanks. I am kinda proud—I guess. Not that I did anything to deserve it."

Ms. Fornello looks me in the eye. "Of course you did," she says. This makes no sense at all. But who am I to argue? Instead of getting punished, I have been rewarded. Unless being an open-house greeter involves some kind of *utter humiliation* I have not figured out yet.

My class is in the computer lab. A tenth-grade class is there too, working at the back of the room.

My class is working in pairs at the front of the lab, entering information into spreadsheets. Tanya and Evie are working together. Lily is behind them, looking grumpy, probably because she's stuck with some other girl. Our teacher, Mr. Hansen, is not surprised when I turn up late. "Go ahead and join Trevor," he says.

Nelson is sitting a couple of desks over. He hangs his head when he sees me. When I pass him, I clap his shoulder. "Hey, no hard feelings, okay?"

"Okay," Nelson says without looking up.

I could apologize. How hard would it be to say I'm sorry? But at the last second I can't resist the opportunity to make another crack. "Nice boxer shorts, by the way." Even Nelson's partner giggles.

Trevor is checking out photos of swimsuit models. "Does that have anything to do with our assignment?" I ask when I sit down next to him.

"'Course not, bro. I was just waiting for you to show up. What's your punishment? Hard labor in the schoolyard? An essay on what Kryptonite can teach humanity?"

"That's the weird part," I tell Trevor. "I didn't get punished. I got *rewarded*.

Principal Owen asked me to be an official greeter at the open house next month. Apparently, it's a big honor."

"You're kidding."

"Nope."

"Did you get Luke's phone back?"

"Yup. But Fornello deleted the video."

"I knew it," Trevor says. "But hey, no biggie. I'll never forget those Superman boxer shorts. You were magnificent, Daniel."

I am basking in the compliment when Mr. Hansen catches my eye. "Boys," he says. He must sense we were not discussing spreadsheet cells.

I nudge Trevor and point to the screen. Mr. Hansen gives an approving nod.

We are supposed to be calculating our weight in space. First we have to enter all the planets. Then we need a new column for each planet's gravity ratio.

We are sharing a computer, and because Trevor is googling gravity ratios and I'm sitting too far away to admire Tanya, I decide to organize my binder. There are a bunch of loose sheets I don't need—old assignments and class notes. "I'm going to dump these in the recycling," I tell Trevor.

The recycling bin is at the back of the lab. I am leaning over to drop the sheets in when I nearly collide with someone coming in from the back entrance to the lab. I suck in my breath when I spot the maroon baseball cap. It's Jeff Kover.

For most of the older students, eighth-graders are mildly annoying. But for Jeff Kover, they are pests he wants to wipe out. He has never picked on me personally. But I have seen him harass other eighth-graders, and it's not pretty.

"Hey, watch where you're going," he mutters.

"I was just…"

But Jeff has already gone to sit down next to Charlotte, this really pretty girl in tenth grade.

Charlotte moves her chair closer to Jeff's. The way she does it makes me wish Tanya would move her chair like that for me. But I almost forget about Tanya when I hear Charlotte ask, "How'd your meeting with Principal Owen go?"

So Jeff was in Principal Owen's office this morning too.

I don't want them to know I am eavesdropping, so I pretend to look for something in my binder.

"It was weird, " Jeff tells her. "Usually when Owen calls me in, it's for a suspension. But today he wanted to know if I'd be a greeter at the open house."

Charlotte punches Jeff's arm. "You? A greeter at the open house? I don't see it. What did you say?"

"I said yes."

"You said yes?" I do not mean to say the words out loud. They just slip out— and Jeff and Charlotte hear me.

I know because they both turn.

"You got a problem with that?" Jeff asks. I can see from his eyes that he is mocking me.

"N-no," I stutter. "I mean, yes. I mean, no. I don't have a problem with that."

Chapter Four

I cannot remember a Saturday I did not work at Handy Hardware. Even in first grade, I used to sweep the floors or dust the bottom shelves. I wasn't tall enough to reach the high ones.

My grandpa founded Handy Hardware in 1960, and now my parents run it. Though the big-box stores and online shopping have changed the business,

Handy Hardware still does okay. Dad says that is because some customers prefer the personal service in a small store.

Ms. Fornello is not the only one with a favorite word. Dad has one too. His word is *branding*. Dad studied marketing at university, and he says Handy Hardware's greatest asset is our brand. That is why instead of updating the store the way most businesses do, Dad does the opposite. He tries to preserve everything that made Handy Hardware special: the bell that chimes when customers walk in, the old-fashioned cash register and the gray aprons we all have to wear.

Now that I'm fourteen, I do a lot more than sweep and dust. I serve customers, mix paint and handle the cash. I make minimum wage, which is decent for someone my age.

We know many of our customers by name. This morning, Milly Burns, who lives on our street, is buying shelving. Milly's daughter got married last year, and Milly wants to turn her daughter's old bedroom into a library. Milly has brought her iPad to show Dad pictures of how she wants the room to look.

"Before you buy the brackets and the shelves," I hear Dad tell her, "I want to send Len by your place to check the walls. Make sure they can handle the weight. Books are heavier than you think."

Len, who has a potbelly and wears thick glasses, has been working at Handy Hardware longer than I've been alive.

I am in the paint section, helping a customer who wants to stain his back deck before it's too cold to do it. "You need to check the weather forecast," I explain. "You'll need two warm, dry days for the stain to take."

I take out my phone to check the forecast. "This weekend doesn't look good.

There's an 80 percent chance of rain tomorrow."

"Well, that sucks," he says, scowling. Something tells me this guy scowls a lot. "You sure it needs two days?"

At the same time as I am discussing wood stain, I keep an eye on a kid in the electrical aisle. Shoplifting cuts into our profits, and something about the kid makes me suspicious. Though you'd be surprised. It isn't only kids who shoplift. We have caught little old ladies and men in business suits red-handed.

"Look, is there someone else I can talk to? Someone with some experience?" the man is saying. He still has that scowl on his face.

There is an edge in the man's voice that does not fit the situation. I decide not to tell him I have plenty of experience. Besides, Dad says the customer is always right. Only this guy isn't right—he's a jerk.

"Of course, sir," I say. "Let me call someone else over. Len?" I call across the aisles. Len is making a key for another customer. "Could you come over here when you're done? I've got a customer who wants some information about wood stain."

The guy does not treat Len any better than he treated me. But I enjoy hearing Len repeat that wood stain needs two days to dry.

"Fine," the man says, slapping his hand on the counter. "The weather had better cooperate next weekend." He makes it sound as if we are responsible for the weather.

If Len finds the customer annoying, he does not let on. "I'm hoping for good weather next weekend myself," Len says with a smile. "The wife wants to go apple picking."

"How much is a gallon?" the man asks.

"Fifty-two dollars," Len tells him.

The man slaps his hand on the counter again—harder this time. "Fifty-two dollars? You gotta be kidding! That's highway robbery."

"That's what stain costs." Len still does not show signs of being rattled.

"Not at a big-box store," the man grumbles.

"Well, you're more than welcome to go to a big-box store." There is nothing angry about the way Len says this. "But ours is good-quality stain. It goes on smooth, and it'll last through our harsh winters."

The man pulls his wallet out of his pocket. I guess he isn't going to bother driving to a big-box store. "At fifty-two bucks a gallon, it better make it through ten winters."

The bell on the front door chimes. When I turn to see who is coming in, I spot a maroon baseball cap. What is Jeff Kover doing here?

Jeff raises a hand in the air. At first I think he recognizes me. But then I realize he is waving at the man who has been giving us a hard time.

"I got here as soon as I could, Dad," Jeff says. *Dad*? Jeff sounds out of breath, nervous. This does not fit with what I know about Jeff. Jeff makes other people nervous.

Jeff's dad wags his finger at his son. "You haven't been on time since the day you were born," he says, shaking his head.

Jeff does not bother to defend himself. Instead, he starts coughing nervously. Could Jeff be scared of his father?

And if so, what would Ms. Fornello say?

Chapter Five

This is our last movie night in the park till next year. Movie nights start in May and go till October, when it gets too cold to sit outside for two hours. They show the movies at Benny Park on the last Sunday of the month.

Everyone brings snacks, and blankets or towels for stretching out on. It's like being on the beach, but with entertainment—and no sand.

People of all ages turn up for movie night. What's funny is how we end up sitting in different sections on the field, kind of like mini neighborhoods. Families with toddlers sit close to the screen, which is the wall of the new community center.

Older people sit on either side of the screen, probably because they are always getting up for pee breaks.

Kids my age sit in the middle. The older kids sit toward the back. The ones with a boyfriend or girlfriend spend more time sucking face than watching the movie.

The movie has already started when Trevor, Luke and I show up. While I look for someplace to sit, I scan the field for Tanya.

Trevor must know who I am looking for because he says, "Over there." I follow his gaze to where Tanya and the side-kicks are stretched out on a plaid blanket. I wish we had gotten here sooner so I could be sharing that blanket too.

I also spot Jeff's maroon baseball cap. I have adjusted my opinion of Jeff since I saw him with his dad at Handy Hardware. It must suck to have such a nasty dad.

Jeff has his arm around Charlotte. If they recognize me, they do not let on. It is not cool for older kids to acknowledge younger ones.

I was hoping for an action film, so I am not thrilled about tonight's movie— some dorky 3-D animation. The main character is an ancient dude who decides he has to visit South America before he drops off the planet. And he's planning to travel there by attaching balloons to his house. Talk about far-fetched.

"This sucks," I tell Trevor and Luke. "I was in the mood for James Bond."

A girl sitting in front of me spins around. She looks about twelve, and she wears her frizzy red hair in a ponytail. She's got one finger pressed to her lips like a teacher. "Shh," she says, glaring at me. "Do you mind keeping it down?"

"As a matter of fact, I do mind," I say. I make a point of speaking more loudly. I know Trevor appreciates my crack because he snorts.

A couple of other kids and some old coot turn around and give Trevor and me the hairy eyeball.

The girl with the ponytail sighs and turns back to face the screen. What bothers me most is the way she acts like she is the older one and we're some kind of pipsqueaks.

Luke stretches out next to me and rests on his elbows. I can tell from the way his mouth hangs open like a dog's that he likes the movie. "This flick's for babies," I say. I'm loud enough to bother the girl again, but she is ignoring me. I lean over to block Luke's view and put my thumb in my mouth.

Luke pushes me out of the way with the back of his hand. Usually he agrees with whatever I say. But not this time. "Check out the wrinkles on the old guy's face," he says, making it sound like Picasso himself painted those wrinkles. "This is first-class animation."

Luke might be right about the animation, but the story still sucks. We are on to flashbacks of the old guy and his wife who died. She is even more wrinkly than the dude.

Trevor has a tub of caramel popcorn propped between his thighs. I grab the tub and stretch out on my blanket. I could try to eat quietly, but I want to annoy Little Miss Ponytail.

"Hey, what do you think you're doing with my popcorn?" Trevor asks.

"Didn't your mother teach you to share?"

Trevor play-swats the side of my head. "I don't call that sharing. I call it stealing."

I am expecting the girl to deliver another lecture, but she just leans in closer to the screen. I can tell from the way she does it that she is making a big effort to tune us out.

The stars are starting to come out. I might as well make the best of a bad situation. The old guy in the movie may not be James Bond, but he has some redeeming qualities. He has a sense of adventure, especially for a senior citizen. Besides, Luke is right—the animation is cool.

Maybe it is not such an awful movie, because I end up getting into it. Things get more interesting when a stowaway kid turns up inside the balloon-powered house.

Ironically, Little Miss Ponytail ends up disturbing *me*. She gets all weepy during the flashbacks when we see the old guy with his wife who died. This girl is the noisiest crier I ever heard. I can hardly hear the movie.

I tap Little Miss Ponytail's shoulder. "Do you mind keeping it down?"

Trevor snorts. I laugh. Luke is too busy admiring the animation to appreciate my awesome sense of humor.

But Little Miss Ponytail pays no attention. Either she is ignoring me or she is so broken up about the old couple in the movie she has forgotten my existence.

When the movie ends, I get up and stretch. In front of me, Little Miss Ponytail is wiping her snotty nose with the back of her hand. When our eyes meet, I remember the way she talked to me before. This is my moment to get revenge—and have some fun.

It's one of those opportunities I can't resist. I nudge Trevor and Luke. I like having an audience.

I gently tap Little Miss Ponytail's shoulder again. I make an effort to sound polite. "Do you mind if I ask you something?"

This time she does not ignore me. "Okay," she says. Even in the dark, I can see that her eyes are bloodshot from crying.

I look over at Trevor and Luke, then back at the girl. "So," I ask her, "are you on the rag or what?"

She gasps and then bursts into slobbery tears. It's one of the funniest things I have ever seen. I don't know who is laughing harder—me or my buds.

I never expected Little Miss Ponytail to get so worked up. Before I can tell her I was only kidding around, she runs out of the park, her ponytail flopping behind her.

Chapter Six

I do a double take at school the next morning when I see Tanya wearing a pink T-shirt with the words *Mean Girl* on it. Talk about stating the obvious.

Tanya winks when she notices me noticing her. "Like my T-shirt?"

"Sure. It's ironic. Everyone knows you're a mean girl." Most guys would be nervous talking to Tanya, but not me.

I'm more confident than your average fourteen-year-old. Besides, Tanya and I have known each other forever. Even back in elementary school, she was mean.

Tanya throws her head back when she laughs. "Are you flirting with me, Daniel Abel?"

"Could be."

Tanya laughs even harder. Which makes me laugh. I like that Tanya thinks I'm funny. "Evie and Lily bought me this T-shirt," she says.

As if on cue, the sidekicks pop their heads out of the girls' bathroom. "C'mon, let's go!" Tanya tells them, and the two girls fall into position, flanking Tanya's sides. "He likes the T-shirt," I hear Tanya say as they head down the corridor. "He called it *ironic*."

I don't want Tanya and her friends to think I am trailing them, because only amateurs let pretty girls know they're crazy about them. So I stop in front of the bulletin board by the main office. There is a poster with a giant louse on it, a notice about the upcoming flu clinic and a poster advertising the open house. That reminds me about my greeter gig. If Jeff Kover was not going to be a greeter as well, I might look forward to it.

Down the hall, Tanya and the side-kicks have planted themselves on the floor near the library. They stretch their legs out in front of them to block the hallway traffic.

I know they are waiting for a victim, the way a spider waits in its web for dinner.

Anyone who wants to go to the library will have to get past the girls' legs. It is no coincidence that they are sitting outside the library's glass double doors. Like a spider wants to attract a tasty bug, Tanya and her friends have set their sights on a certain kind of victim.

Their prey spends recess in the library, not because they have homework but because they don't have a friend in the world. Unless you count the librarian.

From my spot at the bulletin board, I can watch the action unfold.

Abby Lemay is about to become a tasty bug. I know it as soon as I see her close her locker. Abby has three library books. I know because they are covered in crinkly plastic. She must be planning to return the books to the library and spend recess working on some lame assignment that is not due for three weeks. That is how nerds like Abby Lemay roll.

But what will Abby do when she sees Tanya and her friends blocking the way? If Abby turns back, they will know she is a coward. That will make them even meaner the next time they see her.

If Abby keeps walking, she will land smack in their web.

Abby walks briskly. When she slows down, I know she has spotted Tanya and her pals. When Abby comes to a full stop, I can almost feel the gears spinning in her head. She presses the library books to her side—like a shield. Not that those books will do her much good.

Abby looks to the left. Maybe she hopes a teacher is coming down the hall. If a teacher comes by, the girls will have to move their legs. But there is no teacher to save her. Abby looks to the right and over her shoulder. That is when her eyes land on me.

I expect Abby to go back to her locker and wait for a better time to return the books. Girls like Abby will do a lot to avoid confrontation.

I cannot see Tanya's face, but I bet she is smiling.

Then Abby does something that surprises me. She keeps heading straight for the library doors. I start heading there too. I want to see how this goes down.

Abby steps around the girls' legs. One of them—I can't tell which one—squeals. Someone shifts the position of her legs.

Abby trips and stumbles to the floor. When she lands on her back, she is clutching her library books.

Lily and Evie burst into laughter. But not Tanya. She rushes over to help Abby to her feet. Abby has trouble finding her balance. I do not know if it is because she is a klutz or if she has hurt her ankle. "Are you okay?" I hear Tanya ask. She sounds like she cares.

Abby refuses to look at Tanya.

That is when Mrs. Duval, the librarian, appears at the doors, hands on her hips. How much has she seen?

A lot, apparently. Because first she asks Abby if she is all right. When Abby rubs her ankle and whimpers, Mrs. Duval says, "I want you to report to the nurse's office." Now she spots me. "Daniel, Abby is going to need a hand getting to the infirmary."

Mrs. Duval points at Tanya, Lily and Evie. "You three—get yourselves to Principal Owen's office. Now!"

Chapter Seven

Abby hangs on to my elbow as she hobbles down the hallway. "Hopefully, it's just a sprain," I tell her.

When Abby does not answer, I wonder if she is upset with me.

"Does it hurt?" I ask her.

When Abby still does not answer, I decide I was right about her being upset.

"Don't be mad at me. I had nothing to do with what happened out there."

"I saw you watching." Abby spits out the words. I don't argue. But Abby is not done dissing me. "You have a crush on Tanya. And you're a bully like her." I also can't argue about having a crush on Tanya. Every guy in our grade has a crush on Tanya. But calling me a bully—that isn't right.

"If I was a bully, I wouldn't be helping you."

"You're only helping me because Mrs. Duval told you to."

"That's not true. I'd have helped you anyhow." As soon as the words are out of my mouth, I wonder if they are true. "Anyway," I say, "I'm not a bully. Not like Jeff Kover."

Abby tightens her grip on my elbow when I mention Jeff Kover's name.

"Only a bully would *pants* Nelson Wong. Or imitate the way Jason misses the basketball net. Or tease Ronnie about his acne."

What is this girl—some kind of school spy? "For the record," I tell her, "in all those cases, I was only kidding around."

We are almost at the infirmary. Abby lets go of my elbow. She has to hop on one foot to keep her balance. But I get the feeling she would rather hop than rely on my help. "I bet that's what Jeff Kover says too. Did it ever occur to you, Daniel, that Jeff Kover is two years older than us? In two years, you'll be as big a bully as he is. Possibly bigger."

What makes Abby think she has the right to talk to me like that? I am tempted to leave her hopping on one foot like a lame seagull, but I made a promise to Mrs. Duval. So instead of arguing, I follow Abby to the infirmary.

The air smells like rubbing alcohol. A cardboard clock on the door says the nurse will be back in five minutes. When I try to help Abby sit down on one of the chairs outside the office, she waves me away. "I'll wait with you till the nurse gets back," I tell Abby. Then I settle into the other chair.

Abby ignores me.

I grab a pamphlet from the rack behind us. But when I see it is an ad for an anti-bullying hotline, I shove it back into my pocket. Abby must have noticed the pamphlet, because she makes a *harrumphing* sound. Does that mean she is talking to me again?

For a second our eyes meet. If she wasn't so cranky, I might think Abby was pretty. Not in a showy way like Tanya, but in a way a kid might miss if he was not paying attention.

I spot another chair down the hall. I bring it over and set it down in front of Abby. "You should keep your foot elevated," I tell her.

Abby winces when she lifts her foot and rests it on the chair.

"I told you I'm not a bully."

"Just because you say you aren't a bully doesn't mean you aren't one."

I am still thinking about those words when the nurse, Miss Lodge, turns up.

"What did you do to your foot?" Miss Lodge asks Abby.

"I didn't *do* anything to it," Abby answers. "Some girls did. They tripped me. Of course, if you ask them, they'll probably say they were *just kidding around*." I know that last bit is meant for me.

Abby is wearing black work boots. Miss Lodge kneels down to help Abby take off the right one. Abby's face goes white when Miss Lodge pulls down her sock. "It's badly swollen," the nurse says. "Are you able to put weight on it?"

"Some, but it hurts. I had to lean on him"—Abby glances in my direction—"to get over here."

"That was kind of you," Miss Lodge says to me.

I nod as if to say, *Kind is my middle name*.

But Abby does not let me enjoy the moment. "Daniel wasn't being kind," she says. "Mrs. Duval made him help me. We've been in the same class since fourth grade, and this is the first time he's ever said a word to me."

The same class since fourth grade? Really? I had no idea.

Miss Lodge shifts her attention from Abby's ankle to me. "Is that so?"

Because I can't tell whether Miss Lodge expects an answer, I decide not to say anything.

Miss Lodge gets up to unlock the infirmary door. From my seat in the hallway, I see her reach into a mini refrigerator. A minute later she is back with an ice pack. "It looks to me like a bad sprain," she tells Abby. "I'm going to give you some ibuprofen. You're not allergic, are you? Elevating your foot was a good idea—that should help bring the swelling down."

"Elevating her foot was my idea," I say, but neither of them is listening to me.

Miss Lodge returns to the infirmary and comes out with a cup of water and an ibuprofen tablet for Abby. Then she says, "If you don't mind my asking, what happened to the girls who tripped you?"

"The librarian sent them to the principal's office."

Miss Lodge nearly forgets the glass of water in her hand. She lets it hover in midair like a seat on a stalled Ferris wheel. "How many girls did you say there were?"

"Three," Abby and I answer at the same time.

The cup is still hovering in midair. "Does one of them have long black hair? Queen-bee type?"

"That's Tanya," Abby says. "Queen bee is right. That girl stings."

"Interesting," Miss Lodge says, and then she remembers the cup—and puts it down on the floor.

"Why interesting?" I ask.

"Interesting because I was just passing Principal Owen's office. There were three girls waiting outside. It sounds like one of them was your friend Tanya. Principal Owen mentioned they were going to be assisting me at the flu clinic."

"Assisting you at the flu clinic?" Abby says. "That doesn't sound like much of a punishment."

Miss Lodge sighs. "To be honest, that's exactly what I was thinking."

Chapter Eight

"Who do you think those people are?" Trevor asks when we are walking into school the following week.

"Check out the matching computer bags," Luke whispers. "They must be part of some team."

Going up the front stairs ahead of us are two middle-aged women and a guy with a goatee who looks a lot younger.

When we pass them, the visitors turn to look at us. One of the women says hello.

"Uh, who are you guys?" Trevor asks. Leave it to Trevor to blurt that out. Still, I'm curious to know the answer.

The women exchange a look, and then one of them says, "We're researchers from the University of Montreal."

"What exactly are you researching?" Trevor wants to know.

This time the other woman answers. "I'm afraid that's confidential."

The visitors file into the main office, and we head for our lockers. When we get there, Tanya is doing a pirouette. She is wearing a white lab coat. Lily and Evie are clapping; they are in lab coats too. That's when I remember it is flu-shot day. It's not just for students, but for the whole neighborhood. Tanya, Lily and Evie are assisting Miss Lodge. Those three got themselves a sweet deal. They will get to miss all their classes. Too bad the open house is on a Thursday night. Not to mention I'll be stuck with Jeff.

Usually we have to go to the doctor's office for a flu shot. This is the first time the shots are being offered at school. I hope Tanya administers my injection.

Then something occurs to me. This must be why the researchers from the University of Montreal are here. To observe the new flu-shot program. But why are they being so secretive about it?

Our first class is English. We are reading *Lord of the Flies* by William Golding. The beginning is slow, and the writing is old-fashioned. The novel was published in 1954, before my parents were born. Even if it is a classic and won the Nobel Prize, I still think Miss Thompson could have come up with something more current.

Today, Miss Thompson wants to focus on the opening paragraph. I didn't think there was much to it. It said something about a boy with fair hair. But Miss Thompson's eyes light up as she shares her opinion on first paragraphs. "Picture yourselves in the library. You pick up a book because you like the title or the cover. Then you crack it open and read the first paragraph." Miss Thompson holds up an imaginary book and pretends to read from it. Now she tosses the imaginary book into the air. "If the first paragraph doesn't grab you, deal's over."

"Unless it's for school," I call out. "Then you have to keep reading. Unless you don't mind flunking the comprehension quiz."

Everyone laughs, even Miss Thompson. Sometimes all you have to do to make people laugh is point out the obvious.

Miss Thompson waits for the class to settle down, then reads the first paragraph of *Lord of the Flies*. Maybe it's her voice, so calm it's eerie, but this time, I picture the scene. A fair-haired boy heads for a lagoon. He is carrying his school sweater in one hand when he hears a *witch-like cry*.

Miss Thompson only reads that paragraph. When she is done, she does not say anything at all. Maybe she wants the words to do whatever it is words are supposed to do. The room is so quiet, I can hear Luke breathing at the next desk.

Miss Thompson reaches into the giant purse she always carries with her and takes out a pink-and-white seashell the size of a kitten. She beams like a magician who has just pulled a rabbit out of his hat or a quarter from behind his ear.

"If you've done your homework and finished reading chapter one, you'll know why I've brought this to class," Miss Thompson says.

Abby raises her hand. "It's a conch. Like the one the boys in the book use to summon each other."

I'm thinking how *summon* is an unnecessarily fancy word. Why didn't Abby just say *call each other*?

But Miss Thompson is fine with Abby's word choice. "That's right," she says. "I thought we'd spend the rest of today's class discussing the symbolism of the conch. I'll pass my conch around the room—to inspire our discussion."

When Luke gets the conch, he treats it like a cell phone. "Hello, hello! Anybody there? Now if only you came with a built-in camera."

When it is Abby's turn, she holds the conch to her ear and closes her eyes.

"Daniel," Miss Thompson says, "what do you think the conch symbolizes?"

I don't know why she has to call on me. "Uh, the ocean, I guess."

"Yes, the ocean—and by that, I suppose you also mean the natural world."

"Right, that's exactly what I meant. The natural world."

"Abby," Miss Thompson says, "you mentioned how the boys use the conch to summon each other. Would you care to elaborate?"

I can tell from the way Abby straightens her back that she likes getting called on by teachers. "The conch could symbolize human communication."

"*Human communication*." Miss Thompson repeats the words, then pauses the way she did after she read the first paragraph. "That's one of the things that makes us human. Our ability to communicate through language. We can use language to hurt others"—for some reason, my mind flashes on Jeff's father—"or to try to make the world a better place. I think William Golding believed the choice was up to us."

Chapter Nine

My flu-shot appointment is at recess. Because so many people are coming, the clinic is held in the gym. There is a long line when I get there. Some of the people ahead of me are students, and others are from the neighborhood.

Evie and Lily are seated behind a long narrow table, ticking off names on a list.

The three researchers hover in the background. The young guy scribbles notes on a clipboard. So I was right—they are studying the flu clinic.

"Abby Lemay." I look up when Abby says her name. I didn't notice her in line before. She shifts her weight from one foot to another. Maybe her ankle is still sore. Or maybe it is hard for her to face Evie and Lily after what happened outside the library.

"Abby Lemay." Nothing about the way Evie says Abby's name suggests they have history. "If you could read this release form and sign...oh my god!" Evie backs her chair away from the table.

Lily turns to Evie. "Oh my god *what*?"

"She has lice," Evie says, pointing at Abby. "I just saw two crawling around in her hair." She wriggles her index finger to demonstrate.

Abby brings her hand to her scalp, then changes her mind and lets it drop back to her side. "What do I do?" she whispers.

"You need to use coal-tar shampoo. It destroys your hair, but it'll kill the lice. Are you itchy?" Lily asks. The concern in Lily's voice makes me suspicious.

"I wasn't itchy before," Abby says, "but I am now." She brings both hands to her head and scratches.

As soon as Evie covers her mouth, I know the whole thing is a joke. That's when I decide to step out of my spot in line and do something. "Lemme see your scalp," I say to Abby. Abby blushes, but then she leans down so I can have a look. "You don't have lice," I tell her. "Those two are just kidding around."

"I don't?" Abby is so relieved, she forgets to be angry.

Lily and Evie are giggling. "He's right. We were just kidding, Abby," Evie manages to say.

"You shouldn't be so gullible," Lily adds.

Abby smooths her hair. I'm expecting her to give Lily and Evie a lecture about kidding around when an older woman who is next in line clears her throat. "I don't know what you young people think is so funny, but I'd like to get my flu shot before the end of the year."

"Yes, ma'am, we're just waiting for this girl to sign her form," Lily says. She turns back to Abby and taps the spot on the sheet where Abby is supposed to sign.

Abby signs and slides the form across the table. "You two will get your comeuppance," she mutters.

I shake my head. I don't know why Abby had to use a word like *comeuppance*.

Evie is giggling again. "*Comeuppance*?" she says to Lily. "That's what happens when you live in the reference section—you talk like a British dictionary."

"I don't even know what *come-uppance* means," Lily says.

When it is my turn, Evie ticks me off the list. Lily hands me the release form.

"Where's Tanya?" I ask them.

"With Miss Lodge," Evie says. "We each get a turn to shadow her."

"But we'll be sure to let Tanya know you were asking for her," Lily says. "That'll make her day."

"Really?" I say.

"Really." I can't tell from Lily's voice if she is teasing. I hope not.

There is another long table at the side of the gym. This one has a paper tablecloth and is covered with fruit plates, a pyramid of cheese cubes, and juice boxes. "Are those snacks for us?" I ask Lily when I hand her back the form.

"They're for *after* your shot. No allergies, right?" Lily asks as she scans the sheet. I half expect her to make another crack about Tanya and me, but she doesn't. Instead, she points to a long row of folding chairs. "Have a seat until your name is called," she says. Then she looks up at the woman behind me. "Good morning, ma'am. Name, please…" Lily is so professional and polite, I bet the woman would never guess she is talking to one of the meanest girls in our grade.

The researcher with the clipboard comes to stand closer to Evie and Lily. He jots something down. When I try to see what he has written, he puts his palm over it.

"I guess all that is top secret," I say, and he nods.

I take a seat. Because I have nothing better to do, I check out the other people waiting for their flu shots. I don't see Abby. She must already have had hers. A father is talking to his daughter, stroking the side of her head and telling her it will be over before she knows it.

The girl sniffles and tucks her head into the crook of her father's elbow. "Tell her about the snacks," I say to the father, and he mouths the word *thanks* to me. "Sweetheart," he tells the little girl, "that nice young man just reminded me that there are snacks. Do I see strawberries over there?" The little girl lifts her head to peek at the table.

I have been called a *nice young man* before. Usually it happens when I am helping customers at Handy Hardware and I *have* to be nice. This could be the first time anyone ever used those words to describe me at school. I'm glad Trevor and Luke are not around. What would they think?

"Daniel Abel." Tanya calls my name. She looks amazing, even in that lab coat. I nearly tell her so, but then I remind myself you don't let girls like

Tanya know you're crazy about them. They could use it against you.

Tanya gestures for me to follow her to a part of the gym that has been curtained off and asks me to sit at a small desk. I hear Miss Lodge speaking to someone in another curtained-off area nearby. "First your daddy gets his shot, and then it'll be your turn," she says. "Roll up your sleeve, please," she tells the dad.

"One, two—" Before Miss Lodge can count to three, I hear someone retching. I figure it's the little girl. The sour smell of vomit fills my nostrils. For a second, I think I might vomit too.

"Tanya!" Miss Lodge calls out— not in her usual calm voice. "Get some paper towels. Now!"

Tanya swallows. I worry she is about to cry—or vomit. But she exhales and says, "I'm on it."

"I need Lily and Evie too!" Miss Lodge shouts.

Tanya sprints across the gym, past me and the other people waiting their turns. "Lily! Evie!" she calls out, "Miss Lodge needs you." Tanya hurries toward the closest bathroom. The back of her lab coat rises up like the tail wing on an airplane.

I watch her fly past the researcher with his clipboard. "What's going on?" I hear him ask, but Tanya does not stop to answer. A couple of minutes later she is back with a bundle of paper towels. Lily and Evie are already there.

Maybe assisting at the flu clinic has turned out to be a punishment after all. Maybe there *is* such thing as comeuppance.

Chapter Ten

Principal Owen sends me an email. I have to attend a training session for my job at the open house after school today. So much for my plan to hang out with Trevor and Luke. Instead—and my stomach lurches at the thought—I'll be hanging out with Jeff.

Ms. Fornello and Principal Owen are training us. We have to report to Ms. Fornello's office at three thirty.

When I arrive, the researchers from the University of Montreal are leaving. Haven't they finished studying the flu clinic? Are they still tabulating results? I know better than to ask.

"Hi there, Daniel," the guy with the goatee says when he sees me.

I say hi back. What I don't say is, *How come you know my name?*

Jeff comes strolling down the hall. "I'm here," he announces, adjusting his baseball cap.

Principal Owen is in Ms. Fornello's office. He gets up to shake our hands. All this handshaking with a principal makes me nervous. But not Jeff. He pumps Principal Owen's hand like a politician looking for votes.

"How ya doing?" Jeff asks. I guess if you get suspended enough times, you get chummy with the administration.

"You'll be shaking a lot of hands at open house," Ms. Fornello says. "But you should be aware that some people prefer not to shake. They worry about germs," she adds. "Follow their lead. Extend your hand, but watch for their reaction." Ms. Fornello extends her hand to demonstrate, and I automatically shake it.

"Lemme test your handshake," Jeff says. He squeezes my hand so hard my eyes tear up. But I don't say anything. I don't want to give him the satisfaction of letting him know it hurt.

"Dust allergy," I say as I wipe my eyes with the back of my hand.

Jeff grins.

Principal Owen says it's important that we look presentable at open house. "No jeans. No T-shirts with rude slogans." He turns to Jeff. "No baseball caps. I want you two to think of yourselves as ambassadors of Mountview High School."

I catch Jeff's eye when Principal Owen says *ambassadors*. Does Jeff think this is as weird as I do? But Jeff just grins again.

"Ms. Fornello and I have prepared a list of talking points for you—the things that make our school special," Principal Owen continues. "The fact that our students' scores on final exams are among the highest in the province; the multicultural environment; the many clubs students can join, such as the chess club"—Principal Owen turns to Jeff again—"and the weight-lifting club."

"Right," Jeff says, throwing back his shoulders.

Ms. Fornello wants to discuss security. "Since you two are going to be at the front entrance, you'll be the eyes and ears of this school."

Jeff and I follow Principal Owen and Ms. Fornello to the main entrance. "That's where you two will be standing," he says, pointing to the landing at the top of the stairs. He also points out the emergency exits, the fire alarm and the fire extinguishers.

Ms. Fornello shows us the emergency telephone. "If you pick up that phone, security will be here in minutes," she explains.

After we're done, Jeff and I walk out of the building together, and Jeff says, "I heard you pantsed that Asian kid. The one who was wearing Superman shorts. Nice job."

"Thanks. I can't take credit for the shorts though. Hey, there's something I've been meaning to ask you—if you don't mind…"

"Fire away."

"Well, what did you do to…you know…to be a greeter at open house?"

"I stepped on some kid's glasses," Jeff says, waving his hand like it was no big deal.

"Was it an accident?"

"Of course not." Jeff sounds annoyed—like I've insulted him.

"Did you ever read *Lord of the Flies*? In the story, they break one lens of this kid's glasses. His name's Piggy."

"*Lord of the Flies*? That's on the grade-eight reading list, right? I gave up on page two. Too many big words."

I don't tell Jeff I am getting into the book. Instead, I change the subject. Quickly. "Can you believe they made us stay after school for training? Don't they know we've got better stuff to do?"

"Better than getting in good with Principal Owen and Ms. Fornello?" Jeff says. "You know what your problem is, little buddy—you need to look at the long-term benefits."

"Long-term benefits?"

Jeff laughs as if I've said something really funny. "That's right. Long-term benefits. Can't you see what they are up to? They're trying to reform us. If we let them think their plan is working, we're gonna be able to pull off something really big…" Jeff's eyes shine when he says that.

"Really big? What exactly have you got in mind?"

Jeff claps my shoulder. "I haven't figured that out yet. But I can tell you one thing, little buddy. You're gonna be part of it."

I can't decide whether that is good or bad.

I don't want Jeff for an enemy. But I'm not sure I want him for a friend.

Chapter Eleven

1-800-END-MEAN.

I never planned to phone the hotline. But tonight, lying in bed thinking about how Jeff said I was going to be part of his scheme, I remember that the pamphlet I shoved in my pocket is on my dresser now. Next thing I know, I am dialing 1-800-END-MEAN. A man answers, saying,

"You have reached the End Mean hotline." I almost hang up.

I guess I am not the first kid to think about hanging up, because the man says, "Wait! Don't hang up. My name's Theo. I'm here to help you."

So I do not hang up. But I also do not tell him about Jeff. "I'm not calling for me," I say. "I'm calling on behalf of a friend. She's being bullied. I thought maybe, well, maybe you could help me help her."

I hear a phone ringing in the background. I imagine the anti-bullying hotline headquarters—a giant warehouse full of desks with people like Theo answering phones around the clock. If their posters are in every school in North America, they must get a lot of callers.

"That's nice of you to think about your friend. You sound like a kind person," Theo says.

I feel a little guilty when he says that. "I could have done more to help her," I tell Theo. I did not plan to admit this. But when I dialed the hotline number, I didn't really know what I was going to say.

Theo does not seem to think it's strange that I am calling about a friend. Maybe other kids do that too. "Why don't you tell me your friend's name? And your name while we're at it?"

"This call is completely confidential, right?" I whisper. My parents are asleep, and I don't want to wake them. I also don't want them to know I am calling the hotline. They'd only worry.

"Absolutely. Look, you don't have to tell me your name or your friend's— but we've found it helps establish a connection. That's why I told you my name—Theo." Theo has a slow, deliberate way of speaking, as if he has said the same things many times before but still believes they matter.

"Did you ever get bullied, Theo?" The question just pops out.

I am expecting Theo to point out that I've changed the subject and that I still have not told him my name, but he doesn't say either of those things. "I did get bullied. Pretty viciously—but it was a long time ago. That's why I volunteer at the hotline. Because it would have helped me to have a safe place to turn to back then."

I prop myself up on my pillow. "Abby—that's my friend—she's getting bullied at school by these three girls, Tanya"—I pause for a second, because I am picturing Tanya's pale-blue eyes and black hair—"Evie and Lily. Tanya's the ringleader. Evie and Lily just follow along. One of them tripped Abby when she was trying to return library books. Another time they convinced her she had lice. That really freaked Abby out. She got all itchy."

I know I am babbling, but Theo does not stop me. Which makes me want to tell him more. "I'm the one who told Abby the girls were just kidding—that she didn't have lice."

"Standing up like that couldn't have been easy," Theo says. "I'm impressed by your courage. Were you also around when they tripped Abby?"

I am glad Theo does not see me wince.

"Uh, yeah, I was around." I readjust the pillow again. "I was watching."

I can hear Theo breathing on the other end of the phone. "That makes you what we call the *witness*. It's not easy being a witness to bullying either. Do you want to talk about that first, or do you want to talk about ways to support Abby?" he asks.

"Let's talk about Abby," I say, even though I wanted to hear more about the witness part.

"Are you and Abby good friends?" Theo asks.

"To be honest, not exactly. She's not the kind the girl you notice, like Tanya is. But after the tripping incident, the librarian asked me to take Abby to the nurse's office, and we got to talking. Abby's okay. Smart and kind of feisty. She could have turned away when she saw the girls with their legs stretched out in the hallway, but she didn't. That took courage."

"Just like it took courage for you to tell Abby she didn't have lice." Theo pauses. "Have you considered speaking to Tanya or her friends? Telling them to lay off Abby?"

"I couldn't do that."

"You sound very certain," Theo says, but he does not push me further.

Maybe because he does not push me, or because my room is so dark, I end up telling Theo more. "I haven't just been the witness," I admit. "I've been a bully too."

My voice is quieter than a whisper, but I know Theo has heard me, because he says, "I see." I figure he'll start asking me a million questions, but he does not say a word.

"I'm usually just kidding around, but I guess sometimes I end up hurting people. Now there's this guy they've teamed me up with at school. He's two years older, and he's a real bully. I'm afraid he's going to make me do something bad."

"*Make* you do something bad?" Theo repeats my words, turning them into a question. "Do you really think someone can *make* you do something bad?"

I don't answer right away—because I'm not sure. "I guess I need to think about that," I tell Theo.

When I put my phone on the dresser, I only have one regret. I should have told Theo my name.

Chapter Twelve

On the night of open house my parents drop me off on their way to a movie. Mom reaches over to pat my shoulder. "You look nice," she says. She is not used to seeing me with my shirt tucked in.

Dad puts on the hazards so other drivers will know to drive around us. "It's a big honor to represent your school," he adds. "We're proud of you, Daniel."

I don't want them to know I am getting choked up. "Enjoy the movie," I manage to say as I slide the van door shut behind me.

Jeff is getting out of another van. I spot his dad scowling behind the wheel. Jeff shuts the door without saying goodbye. Then the van screeches down the street. Another driver rolls down her window and shouts, "Slow down! This is a school zone!" But Jeff's father is already halfway down the block.

Jeff and I leave our coats in our lockers. Jeff taps the inside pocket of his parka. "I've got a little surprise in here for you," he says. I am about to ask him what he has when Ms. Fornello walks in. She gives us each a laminated pin with our name printed on it in raised letters. Jeff pins his onto the blue-and-white checked shirt he is wearing. I pin mine on too.

The school could have given us paper name tags. Maybe this means Jeff and I will be asked to be greeters again.

The open house does not officially start for another half hour, but the halls are already jammed. I spot Nelson and some of his friends in front of a display for the math club. I nearly collide with Abby, who explains that she is helping in the library. Tanya, Evie and Lily are here too. Tanya flips her hair when she sees me. I hope it means she likes me. "We're assisting Miss Lodge—in case of emergency," Tanya explains.

"Let's just hope no one vomits," Evie adds.

Luke is shooting video for the school website. I even spot the researchers from the University of Montreal. Maybe the two women are considering sending their kids to Mountview next year. But that doesn't explain why the guy with the goatee is also here. He's too young to have kids in our school.

I join Jeff at the top of the front stairs. Ms. Fornello is there too.

A crowd makes its way up the stairs toward us. The kids look small, though they are only two years younger than I am. I remember coming to the open house when I was their age and feeling scared and out of place. "Hello," I say, extending my hand, "welcome to Mountview High School. I'm Daniel Abel."

Jeff is greeting people next to me. I figure he is not crushing anyone's fingers because I don't hear any groans or see anyone's eyes tear up.

When I catch Ms. Fornello's eye, she smiles. The researcher with the goatee passes by to have a word with her. Though they appear to be deep in conversation, I can tell Ms. Fornello is still supervising us.

Jeff and I spend the first half hour shaking hands and directing visitors to the auditorium, where Principal Owen will be speaking about school policies. When my mouth gets dry, I tell Jeff I need a sip of water.

A girl with red hair is standing by the fountain with her parents. "That guy who was at the top of the stairs when we came in—he's a bully," I hear her say.

I clear my throat. I want to tell them that once you get to know Jeff, he is not so bad. Principal Owen would never have asked him to be a greeter if he did not believe Jeff was capable of change. "Um, excuse me…" I say.

When the girl sees me, her eyes widen. That is when I realize she was talking about me.

The girl backs away.

"Look," I say, "I think you're confusing with me somebody else."

But now I know I have seen this girl before. At movie night. I teased her for crying about the old couple in the movie. Didn't I say something about her being on the rag? Now I wish I'd kept my big mouth shut.

I shift my weight from one foot to the other. "Look," I say to the girl. "I'm sorry."

She looks right at me. "What for?"

I can feel my Adam's apple twitch. "For teasing you."

I can tell from the way she is looking at me that she is waiting for me to say more. I take a deep breath. I hate these kinds of conversations. "For asking if you were on the rag. I shouldn't have done that."

"My grandmother died in August. That's why I got so upset during the movie," the girl says. "Not because I was on the rag." She says *on the rag* in a harsh, sarcastic way I know is meant as an imitation of me. Did I really sound so mean?

"I said I was sorry. And I'm sorry about your grandmother. That must be tough."

The girl's parents are taking in every word of this conversation. "What I don't understand," the mother says, "is why anyone would ask a boy like you to greet visitors tonight."

"Because I'm trying to turn over a new leaf." My mouth feels even drier than before. I lean over the fountain and take a giant gulp of water. The redheaded girl watches me. She shakes her head. I guess she doesn't have much faith in my being able to turn over a new leaf.

"Everything okay?" Ms. Fornello asks when I report back for duty. "You look a little off."

"I'm fine."

"Well then, boys, I'm going to need to leave you two on your own for a few minutes. I promised Principal Owen I'd join him in the auditorium." Ms. Fornello looks first at me, then at Jeff, and then she gives us a big smile. "You've both been doing a wonderful job tonight. I know I can trust you to keep up the good work."

"You can trust us," I say, mostly because I can tell she expects an answer.

"Sure," Jeff says.

Ms. Fornello does not notice that Jeff has nudged me with his elbow.

"Trust us?" Jeff says as soon as Ms. Fornello is out of earshot. "That's a good one. Hey, I think it's time for your surprise."

Jeff heads back to his locker, leaving me to be the sole greeter on duty. I try to concentrate on shaking hands and pointing people toward the auditorium, but I am distracted. I'm wondering about Jeff's surprise. Something tells me that whatever it is, Principal Owen and Ms. Fornello are not going to like it.

Jeff returns with a small package wrapped in brown paper. He tosses the package at my face. I catch it, and when I tear it open, my heart sinks. Inside is a satiny red-and-blue Superman cape.

"That Asian friend of yours is doing his presentation in ten minutes. With this cape on, he's gonna look like a bona fide superhero," Jeff says.

I think about my conversation with Theo from the hotline. *Do you really think someone can* make *you do something bad?* I also think about the way the redheaded girl shook her head at me. "Maybe we should leave Nelson alone," I say quietly.

Jeff claps my shoulder so hard I have to rub it. "What are you, some kind of wuss?" he asks. He grins when he sees me rub my shoulder. "Besides," he adds, "you and me, we have something in common. We both like kidding around."

Chapter Thirteen

I do like kidding around. But there is something I really *don't* like. I don't like being called a wuss.

But I am not into bullying Nelson.

"Why don't *you* do it?" I know that by now everybody at school has forgotten how Nelson was wearing Superman boxer shorts the day I pantsed him. But the Superman cape will remind them. Nelson will be humiliated all over again.

There is no point in appealing to Jeff's sense of decency. Because I don't think he has one.

"I'm gonna be too busy," Jeff says.

"Busy doing what?"

Jeff rolls his eyes. "Do I have to tell you everything?"

"Aren't you afraid of getting into trouble?" Jeff doesn't answer, and I'm getting desperate, so I ask, "Don't you ever think about turning over a new leaf?"

"Me?" Jeff says, when he finally stops laughing. "Afraid of getting into trouble? I *enjoy* getting into trouble. And no, I never thought about turning over *a new leaf*!"

"Wouldn't you like to be a school greeter again?" I ask.

Now Jeff has to hold on to his stomach to control his laughter. "Of course

I wouldn't like to be a school greeter again! Being a school greeter is for wusses. Don't you see what they're up to, Danny-boy?"

"Up to? What are you talking about? Who's up to anything?"

"We're part of some wacky experiment. That's why those researchers have been crawling around school like centipedes. Centipedes with notebooks," he says, glancing over his shoulder at the guy with the goatee. Sure enough, he is jotting something in his notebook.

"I thought they were researching the flu clinic. Did you hear how three girls from my grade got stuck mopping up some kid's vomit?"

Jeff shakes his head like he is tired of having to explain things to idiots like me. "Let me ask you something. Those three girls—weren't they being punished too?"

"I guess."

Jeff claps my shoulder. I wish he'd quit doing that. "I thought you were smart, Danny-boy." I also wish he would stop calling me Danny-boy. "Instead of punishing bad behavior, Owen's *rewarding* it. It's some kind of twisted experiment to see how we'll react. I'll bet you anything Ms. Fornello is behind it. She's trying to change us. Do you enjoy being treated like a laboratory rat? Because I don't. Now will you do me a favor and throw this cape over your friend's shoulders?"

The guy with the goatee is still scribbling. I agree with Jeff about one thing. I don't like being treated like a laboratory rat. Nelson Wong is at the back of the lobby. He is standing at a podium, moving his lips as he reviews his notes. I unfold the Superman cape and drape it over my arm.

Now will you do me a favour and throw this cape over your friend's shoulders?

Jeff's words echo in my head. It's the word *friend* that stops me. Not that Nelson is my friend. He's not my friend any more than Abby is. But why do I feel responsible for them? Would I do something else to humiliate Nelson? Is it worth a laugh?

Jeff pushes me into the crowd toward the math-club booth.

Nelson's eyes widen, and he jerks his head back when he sees me coming. I know it is because he is afraid of me. That fear makes me feel powerful—but also guilty.

An Asian woman stands nearby, filming the crowd with her cell phone. I am close enough to toss the cape over Nelson's shoulders. I can almost hear the other kids laughing.

I extend my arm.

Do you really think someone can make *you do something bad*? Theo's words echo in my head.

I drop my arm to my side and crunch the satiny fabric up into a ball.

Jeff will call me a wuss, but I'll deal with that.

I join the small semicircle of people waiting to hear Nelson's speech. The woman with the cell phone must be Nelson's mom. She moves over to make room for me and nods in a friendly way, like she is glad to see me.

"G-good evening, l-ladies and gentlemen," Nelson stammers, and I wonder if he would be this nervous if I wasn't in the audience. "I've been asked to say a few words about the Mountview High School Math Club. We meet every Wednes—"

But Nelson never finishes, because the fire alarm goes off.

"Fire!" a panicky voice shouts. Other voices join in, shouting, "Fire!"

Someone pushes me toward the main entrance. I look for Jeff, but he is not where I left him at the top of the stairs.

That is when I know Jeff set off the alarm.

Chapter Fourteen

My first thought is, this is fun.

The lobby is total chaos. Voices shouting "Fire!" and "Move!" compete with the clang of the fire alarm. Best of all, there is no sign of Principal Owen or Ms. Fornello. Come to think of it, there are hardly any adults around. They must all be in the auditorium for Principal Owen's talk.

We are like the kids in *Lord of the Flies*. Free to do whatever we choose. Unsupervised.

I make a whooping sound. Other kids copy me, and soon a chorus of wild whooping and laughter fills the air.

Luke is perched on a table someone has dragged to the side of the lobby. He is shooting video. "You rock, Lucas!" I shout. He answers with an air punch.

I feel someone's hand on the small of my back, pushing me deeper into the crowd. "Lay off, will you?" I say, but the kid behind me doesn't hear or doesn't care, because he pushes harder. So I end up pushing forward too. The kid in front of me tries to speed up, but there is no room. The lobby is so packed we can barely turn our heads. Where are the researchers from the University of Montreal? I guess they have finally had to put away their clipboards.

"I smell smoke!" someone cries.

"Do you smell smoke?" kids' voices ask.

I sniff the air—though I am nearly sure it is a false alarm. No smoke. Just armpit stink, probably because kids are getting stressed.

I'm not loving the feeling of being crushed. I try extending my elbows, but there is no room. Someone has a coughing fit. The crowd presses forward like one giant person.

Did I really think this was fun?

Because I've changed my mind.

Everywhere I look, kids are shoving and pushing. When I look down, I see a solid mass of legs and feet. I wipe my forehead. That's when I realize I am sweating too.

I hear more coughing, then wheezing. "He's having trouble breathing!" a worried-sounding voice calls out. But everyone keeps pressing forward. If only someone would shut off the alarm, people might calm down. I press forward too. It's like I am caught in a giant wave. There is no sense in fighting the current. But then the wheezing sounds come closer, and I think, What about the kid who can't breathe?

"It isn't a real fire!" I holler, but no one pays any attention.

I am close enough now to just make out the outline of some kid lying on the floor. He is wearing a blue-and-white checked shirt like the one Jeff was wearing. I know that can't be Jeff on the floor. Jeff masterminded this stampede. I'll bet anything he is somewhere on the edge of the crowd, enjoying the show.

The guy on the floor is wheezing and flailing his arms.

"Do you carry an inhaler for your asthma?" someone asks.

No answer. Just more wheezing and flailing. I don't want to look—and at the same time, I do.

"I think it's an asthma attack," I hear the same voice say. "A serious one. Probably triggered by panic. Kid, can you talk? Where's your inhaler? Don't tell me you don't carry an inhaler!"

No answer. Less flailing. Which is when I realize the guy on the ground is in real trouble.

Now a woman's voice. "Check his pockets. Maybe his inhaler's in there!"

Someone crouches to check the guy's pockets. "Nothing in his pockets!"

The crowd heaves, pushing me even closer to the guy on the floor. I nearly have an asthma attack when I see his face.

That guy gasping for breath?

It's Jeff.

He does not look anything like the Jeff I know. There is a look in his eyes I have never seen there before. Pure fear.

"He's your friend, isn't he?" someone asks me. "Does he carry an inhaler?"

It's Nelson. His mom is next to him. She must have been the one who suggested checking Jeff's pockets.

I want them to know Jeff is not my friend. That we just got stuck together for open house. But there is no time for an explanation.

What I do instead is shout as loudly as I can, "We need an inhaler—now!" This time, my voice carries in the crowd. I didn't even know my voice could do that.

Before, kids whooped when they heard me whooping. Now I hear them passing on my message.

It's Nelson's idea to form a circle around Jeff. "It's better if you face out," he explains to the kids who are making the circle. "That will help stop the stampede, and he won't have to worry about getting trampled."

Nelson drops to his knees and tries to prop Jeff up, but Jeff is too heavy. I kneel down to help.

Nelson has also noticed the look in Jeff's eyes because he tells him, "Relax. It's going to be okay."

I wish Nelson sounded a little more sure about that.

Chapter Fifteen

Jeff closes his eyes and tries to take a deep breath. But that only makes him cough again. It's a wheezy, anxious cough. Could Jeff's asthma attack really be triggered by panic? I never thought a kid as big and tough as Jeff could feel panicky. It doesn't compute.

It wouldn't surprise me if a shy, skinny kid like Nelson had panic attacks.

But Nelson is calmly talking to Jeff, trying to help him catch his breath. Lots of stuff is not computing today.

The outward-facing circle was a good idea. Maybe once Jeff realizes he is not in danger of being trampled, he will be able to catch his breath.

"Miss Lodge is on her way!" someone shouts.

I notice Nelson catch his mother's eye and mouth the words, *He needs an inhaler. Or else…*

It's the *or else* that frightens me.

Now I remember that in *Lord of the Flies*, Piggy has asthma too. And Piggy panics. In the book, things really fall apart when the kids are scared. Fear keeps them from thinking straight and acting like a team. I can't let that happen to me. To us.

There was a mountain on the island in *Lord of the Flies*. If only there were some kind of mountain in the lobby.

If I was higher up than everybody else, they might listen to me.

That's when I get an idea.

What if we make our own mountain—the way circus performers do?

"I have an idea. But I need help." I picture myself at the top of a human pyramid—the hero of open house. Just as I am thinking that, someone pushes his way through the circle. It's Trevor.

"Hey, bud," I say. "You're just in time. We're gonna make a pyramid. I need you to squat at the bottom."

Luckily, Trevor does not object—or ask questions. He drops to the floor, tucking his head between his shoulders.

"We need two more kids for the base of the pyramid," I call out.

Nelson looks up at me and shakes his head. "Do you really expect me and my friends to trust you?" he asks.

Jeff's eyes are closed again, and his eyelids are fluttering. But Nelson is right. Why should he and his friends trust me? "Okay," I tell him. "I'll be part of the base. You can be the guy on top. Just get us an inhaler."

I squat down next to Trevor. Another guy from the math club squats down next to me. I try to concentrate on my breathing and not on the pain when someone else steps on my back. I can feel the soles of his shoes pressing down on either side of my spine.

When Nelson climbs the base of our pyramid and the two guys standing on top of us raise him into the air, I am glad he is so scrawny. Otherwise my back might break.

Nelson's voice is not strong, and at first it doesn't carry in the crowded lobby. But soon the wild throng of kids spots him at the top of our mountain.

Though my head is down and I cannot see Nelson, I imagine him perched over the crowd, waving his arms overhead.

And now I can hear him. Loud and clear, because the crowd has suddenly fallen silent. "A kid here is having a serious asthma attack. Who's got an inhaler?"

"I do!" a faraway voice calls out.

"Pass it! Pass the inhaler here! Hurry!" I hear other kids saying.

Nelson climbs down and the pyramid kids form a circle again and wait for the inhaler. I am doing stretches for my back when it arrives.

Jeff still can't speak, and his face is grayer than ashes, but he manages to bring the inhaler to his lips.

Those of us in the circle watch as he takes two deep inhalations. Almost immediately, his chest stops heaving.

"Who had the inhaler?" Nelson asks when it is clear that Jeff is going to be okay. Miss Lodge has arrived and is checking Jeff's vital signs.

"It was Tanya Leboff's inhaler," some guy answers.

Tanya has asthma?

It's another bit of information that does not compute.

Three fire engines arrive in the circular driveway in front of the school. Within a minute, a dozen firefighters are storming the building. Even underneath their masks, their faces look serious.

Ms. Fornello and Principal Owen arrive in the lobby. First they want to know if Jeff is okay. Then they explain to the firefighters that it was a false alarm.

"Deliberately triggering a fire alarm is an indictable offense," I hear a firefighter tell Principal Owen.

"I'm aware of that," Principal Owen says. "And we'll do our best to find the culprit. But from what I understand, things could have been much worse. We nearly had a stampede in here.

Thank goodness, a core group of decent, responsible students prevailed."

Does Principal Owen really look at me when he says that?

Chapter Sixteen

They are shooting a video at Mountview. A professional videographer is in charge, but Luke is assisting. From the way he is strutting around, you'd think he'd been nominated for an Academy Award. I nearly point that out, but then figure I might as well let Luke enjoy his five minutes of fame.

I got my five minutes after open house. I was even interviewed for an article in the community paper. The reporter wanted to know how I got the idea of making a human pyramid and how I felt when Jeff started breathing normally again. I could tell she liked it when I told her the idea for a pyramid came from reading *Lord of the Flies*. And, of course, I said I was relieved when Jeff was okay.

I never told anyone—not even Trevor and Luke—that I was sure Jeff triggered the alarm. I didn't bring it up with Jeff either. There was not much point. Besides, after everything that happened, Jeff mellowed. He didn't change from a caterpillar to a butterfly, but he stopped picking on younger kids. And kids weren't so intimidated by him anymore. Maybe because word spread that his asthma attack was triggered by panic. If a bully panics, well, he can't be that scary, right?

Jeff and I are sitting together in the front row of the auditorium. Jeff is wearing his checked shirt again. We are both going to be interviewed at the end of the video.

Ms. Fornello invited a bunch of other kids to the filming too. Abby and Nelson Wong are sitting behind us. Tanya, Evie and Lily are huddled together in the back row. Jason and Ronnie, the guys I got in trouble for teasing at the beginning of the school year, are here too.

Ms. Fornello and the researchers from the University of Montreal are up first.

It turns out Ms. Fornello is not only a guidance counselor. She is also working on her PhD in something called educational psychology. Those researchers from the University of Montreal have been working on a project that was Ms. Fornello's idea.

Jeff nudges me. "Didn't I tell you she was the brains behind it?"

Ms. Fornello explains how she came up with the project. "As a guidance counselor, I have seen firsthand that punishing bad behaviors such as bullying often fails to work. Traditionally, researchers have focused on how bullies may themselves be victims of bullying. I'm not saying this never happens. I know it does. I firmly believe that bullies who have or who continue to experience bullying—say, in their homes—need our support." For a moment her eyes meet Jeff's, and for the first time I wonder about the conversations the two of them have in her office.

"However," Ms. Fornello continues, "I've observed that a surprising number of bullies are not what we call *victim-bullies*. In fact, these bullies tend to be successful and popular, and they often possess natural leadership qualities."

I straighten my shoulders when she says that.

"So I wondered what would happen if, instead of punishing bullies, we gave them high-status positions at the school. My hope was that the bullies would rise to the occasion. I ran the idea by my boss, Richard Owen, the principal at Mountview, and he agreed to give it a go. I suppose it's fortunate there was no shortage of bullies at this school."

I let my shoulders slump back down.

Ms. Fornello introduces the other three members of her research team. She also explains how important it was that none of the subjects realized they were part of an experiment.

Jeff nudges me again. "I don't know why she doesn't just go ahead and call us lab rats."

"Had they known they were part of an experiment, they might have altered their behavior," Ms. Fornello says.

The researcher with the goatee is up next. He reports on what happened during the flu clinic. How two subjects tried to bully a classmate, but then when called upon to act as a team with another subject, they did the right thing. He doesn't name names, but we all know who he is talking about. When he finishes his account, Abby sighs. I am disappointed he did not mention the word *vomit*. In my opinion, vomit was the best part of that story.

Mr. Goatee smiles into the video camera as he steps down from the stage. The two women researchers come up next. They are both wearing business suits. The first one explains how two of the school's most active bullies were recruited to participate in the project. She does not mention that we are sitting in the front row. "Instead of punishing them, the two subjects were invited to be greeters at the school's open house. They were told they would be acting as ambassadors of their school."

Her partner takes over the story at this point. She is wearing a pearl necklace. "Initially on the night of open house, our subjects were supervised by Ms. Fornello. It was our plan to leave them alone in order to see what would transpire. At this point, however"—she tugs on her pearls—"things got a little out of hand. In fact, rather than tell you what happened, we're going to show you."

A screen comes down at the back of the stage. I know the video we are about to see was shot by Luke. This is the reason for his Academy Award-nominee routine.

Considering it was shot on a cell phone, the video's not bad.

"That's us!" Jeff calls out. There we are, welcoming visitors to Mountview. Ms. Fornello is there too, looking pleased as she supervises us. And there are the three researchers, scribbling notes on their clipboards.

The camera lands on the redheaded girl, coming up the stairs with her parents. At one point she stops and bites her lip. Was that when she spotted me?

The video moves to the math-club display. Nelson is reviewing his notes. Fast-forward and there I am, crumpling up something in my hand. The Superman cape.

Now we hear the clang of the fire alarm, and we see everyone in the lobby freaking out. I remember how at first I enjoyed the chaos, but how it did not take long before I started to hate the feeling of being pushed by the crowd.

Next to me in the auditorium, Jeff grips the arms of his seat. Is his breathing getting shallower?

"Have you got your inhaler?" I whisper.

Jeff nods. His eyes are glued to the screen.

I know what's about to happen, but this is Jeff's first time seeing it.

There is Nelson, towering over the crowd, asking if someone has an inhaler.

At the back of the auditorium, Evie says to Tanya, "Thank god you had your inhaler with you."

Tanya shushes her. "I'm trying to concentrate on the video."

In the next scene, Jeff is sucking on the inhaler.

The six of us who helped make the human pyramid are watching. I spot the back of my head. I'm between Trevor and Nelson.

I am expecting the camera to pan back to Jeff. If it was my video, I'd end it with Jeff looking grateful and starting to breathe normally. But Luke has done something different for the ending. Something artier.

There's a wide-angle shot of the crowd. Only now, people are calmer.

They have realized it was a false alarm. I think they are also glad that somehow, even in all that chaos, they managed to work together to help Jeff.

The camera does a final sweep over the crowd, landing on the circle of kids who have gathered around Jeff. If I didn't know Abby, she might be just one more face watching the action unfold. But because I know her, my eyes land on her. She is looking at me—almost as if she is seeing me for the first time. Does this mean she was there the whole time, watching while we made the pyramid and got Jeff the inhaler?

The screen goes fuzzy.

A few people in the audience clap, but Ms. Fornello asks them to hold their applause until the end of the presentation. "I'd like to call on two students now. Jeff Kover and Daniel Abel, if you could join me.

"I thought you boys might like to say a few words—about your participation in the project. Jeff, perhaps you could go first?"

Jeff has trouble looking into the camera, so he ends up talking to his feet. "To be honest," he tells his feet, "I didn't like being treated like some lab rat."

I wonder if the researchers are going to edit out that part, but Ms. Fornello is smiling. Which makes me think she really wants our honest opinion.

"If you didn't figure it out yet," Jeff continues, "I'm the kid in the video who was having the asthma attack. I got kind of...well...panicky that night. And if it wasn't for all the kids who pitched in, my story might have had a bad ending, if you know what I mean. I don't want you to think I'm a new person or anything, but...well..." Jeff finally looks up into the camera.

"I feel grateful. And I haven't always been the grateful type."

A spotlight lands on me, and I know it is my turn to say something. I force myself to look into the camera. I raise my voice, not only because I want it be loud enough for the video, but also because I want my friends in the audience to hear me. Not just Tanya, Evie, Lily and Jeff, but also Nelson Wong and Abby, and even Jason and Ronnie. "I guess what I learned from Ms. Fornello's experiment is that I was wrong about a lot of stuff—and a lot of people." I don't mention that one of the people I was wrong about was Jeff, and how I learned that for him, bullying was a way to make people think he was tougher than he really is.

"Mostly I was wrong about myself. I never saw myself as a bully." I turn away from the camera for a moment, because I need to look at Abby when

I say what I am about to say. "I always thought I was just kidding around. I never really thought about the people I was hurting."

Abby nods at me. I'm not quite done. "I guess I discovered something else too. Something pretty important. That it feels good to be in charge sometimes and to be able to help other kids."

Ms. Fornello raises her palm to signal she has something to add. "Thank you, boys. I'd like to wrap up by telling you that we are hopeful our research will help put an end to bullying. We also hope that Jeff and Daniel will join our team as spokespersons to spread the word that change is possible."

Jeff and I exchange a look. We roll our eyes at the same time. Then we shrug. "You don't look too bad," I tell him, "for a butterfly."

ACKNOWLEDGMENTS

A news story about an Arizona school with a new approach to handling bullies inspired me to write *Bullies Rule*. Though I never met Canadian professors Jennifer Wong and Tony Volk, I am grateful to them for their research into bullying and their involvement in the Arizona pilot project. Thanks to Jack Morantz, Spartacus and Junebug for letting me talk to them about this story during our walks together in NDG. Thanks also to my editor and friend Melanie Jeffs, with whom I first discussed this project over dinner in Victoria. As always, I am grateful for Melanie's wise insights, careful reading and great suggestions. Finally, thanks to the whole wonderful team at Orca Books, and to editor Tanya Trafford, for taking *Bullies Rule* to the finish line.

Monique Polak has written many novels for youth, including the Orca Currents titles *Hate Mail* and *Leggings Revolt*. When not writing award-winning books, Monique Polak teaches English and Humanities in Montreal, Quebec, where she also works as a freelance journalist. For more information, please visit www.moniquepolak.com.

1743